ana & Andrew

Family Reunion

the LEWIS family ~ 75th REUNION

by Christine Platt

illustrated by Anuki López

About the Author
Christine A. Platt is an author and scholar of African and African-American history. A beloved storyteller of the African diaspora, Christine enjoys writing historical fiction and non-fiction for people of all ages. You can learn more about her and her work at christineaplatt.com.

For every child, parent, caregiver and educator.
Thank you for reading Ana & Andrew! —CP

To my grandmother Isabel, the kindest and wisest person in the world. —AL

abdobooks.com

Published by Magic Wagon, a division of ABDO, PO Box 398166, Minneapolis, Minnesota 55439. Copyright © 2021 by Abdo Consulting Group, Inc. International copyrights reserved in all countries. No part of this book may be reproduced in any form without written permission from the publisher. Calico Kid™ is a trademark and logo of Magic Wagon.

Printed in the United States of America, North Mankato, Minnesota.
102020
012021

THIS BOOK CONTAINS
RECYCLED MATERIALS

Written by Christine Platt
Illustrated by Anuki López
Edited by Tyler Gieseke
Art Directed by Candice Keimig

Library of Congress Control Number: 2020941578

Publisher's Cataloging-in-Publication Data

Names: Platt, Christine, author. | López, Anuki, illustrator.
Title: Family reunion / by Christine Platt ; illustrated by Anuki López.
Description: Minneapolis, Minnesota : Magic Wagon, 2021. | Series: Ana & Andrew
Summary: Every summer, Ana & Andrew's family gathers in Savannah, Georgia, for a reunion. This year is the 75th anniversary! They go on a road trip, play with their cousins, and learn about the importance of family.
Identifiers: ISBN 9781532139666 (lib. bdg.) | ISBN 9781644945209 (pbk.) | ISBN 9781532139949 (ebook) | ISBN 9781098230081 (Read-to-Me ebook)
Subjects: LCSH: African American families--Juvenile fiction. | Family reunions--Juvenile fiction. | Cousins--Juvenile fiction. | Travel--Juvenile fiction.
Classification: DDC [E]--dc23

Table of Contents

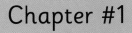

Chapter #1
Countdown to Savannah

Ana and Andrew always enjoyed summer vacation. During the day, they went to camp with their friends. At night, Mama and Papa allowed them to stay up a little later since they didn't have school the next day.

Summer was also when they attended their favorite family event.

"Time to count down!" Andrew said excitedly. "Only one more week until family reunion!"

Ana gave Sissy a big hug. "I can't wait to see our cousins. And Sissy, you're going to see your doll cousins."

Mama pointed to a picture of Ana and Sissy standing with her cousins and their dolls. They were all dressed alike. "You both sure had fun last summer."

"I can't wait to play all day." Andrew thought about how much fun they'd had playing games outside.

Every summer, Papa's family held a reunion in Savannah, Georgia, at Great Uncle Isaac's large farm. Ana and Andrew's family members came from many different states to spend the weekend together. The big celebration was one of the best parts of the summer.

"Hey, this will be Aaron's first family reunion." Andrew held Aaron's hands to help him stand up. "There's a lot of dancing, little brother. So, you better start practicing!"

Andrew did a wiggle dance. And everyone laughed as Aaron tried to do a wiggle dance too.

Ana and Andrew couldn't wait for the rest of their family to meet Aaron, especially their cousins.

"Yes, this family reunion is going to be very special," Papa said. "We have a great deal to celebrate and be thankful for."

Chapter #2
Road Trip

One week later, Ana and Andrew carefully packed their suitcases. There was a lot to do at the family reunion, and they wanted to make sure they had everything they needed.

First, they packed their swimsuits.
The cousins always went swimming in
the lake at Great Uncle Isaac's farm.

The weather in Savannah was
very warm. So, they packed T-shirts,
shorts, socks, and sneakers. Finally,
they packed their favorite pajamas
and toothbrushes.

"Who's ready for our road trip tomorrow?" Papa shouted.

"We are!" Ana and Andrew yelled back to him.

The drive to Savannah was a little over eight hours long. Ana and Andrew passed the time by reading books. They also played fun games like trying to spot cars with license plates from different states. Mama and Papa joined in, especially when they sang songs.

Ana and Andrew called out each state they passed through.

"Virginia!" Andrew said when he saw the state sign.

"Now we're in North Carolina," Ana announced when they crossed into the next state.

In South Carolina, Papa stopped to get gas. Then, they went to their favorite out-of-town restaurant, Miss Amy's Diner. They ate lunch there every summer on their way down South.

"It's the Lewis family!" Miss Amy gave everyone a big hug. "And if y'all are in my diner, that can only mean one thing."

"That's right!" Ana and Andrew said proudly. "It's family reunion time!"

After lunch, Ana and Andrew took a long nap during the car ride. They went to sleep with big smiles on their faces because they knew where they'd be when they woke up: Savannah!

Chapter #3
Family Traditions

"We're here," Mama whispered.

Ana and Andrew yawned and looked out the car windows at Great Uncle Isaac's farm. Their cousins had already arrived and were playing outside.

"Woo hoo!" Andrew said as he unbuckled his seat belt.

Ana saw her cousin Mya sitting on a blanket having teatime with her doll. "C'mon, Sissy. Let's go!"

After a few games, Ana and Andrew went swimming with their cousins. Then, they went to the barn to visit the farm animals. After that, they went inside the house to clean up.

"Do you smell that?" Ana asked Andrew.

"I sure do!" Andrew rubbed his tummy.

Together, they went into the kitchen. Several adults were laughing as they cooked and baked desserts for the big family dinner. Ana and Andrew hugged their grandparents, aunts, and uncles.

21

Aunt Marcie let them each have a sample of her famous pies.

"I just love family reunion." Andrew sighed as he took a bite of sweet potato pie.

"Me and Sissy do too." Ana smiled as she tasted her favorite—apple pie.

That night, everyone went into the living room to listen to Great Uncle Isaac tell stories. He was their oldest family member, and listening to his stories was a tradition.

"This is the 75th anniversary of the Lewis family reunion," Great Uncle Isaac said. "We've been coming together to celebrate since I was a young boy."

"Wow!" Andrew said.

"Yes," Uncle Isaac said. "Fifty years ago, there were just a few family members. But look at us now!"

Everyone looked through photo albums. The pictures from the first family reunions were very old. Ana and Andrew felt very special to be a part of the Lewis family and continue the traditions.

Chapter 4

Let's Celebrate!

Everyone ate breakfast together the next morning. When it was time to get dressed, everyone wore a special gift—a family reunion T-shirt. There was even a little one for Sissy!

While the adults held their family meeting, Ana and Andrew played more games with their cousins and went swimming again. Everyone ate lunch together outside and enjoyed the sunshine.

Then it was time for the family award ceremony.

Mama and Papa received an award for traveling the farthest to attend family reunion. Great Uncle Isaac won an award for being the oldest.

"I have the honor of giving the award to our youngest family member," Great Uncle Isaac said. "And the award goes to . . . Aaron Lewis!"

Ana and Andrew giggled as Aaron tried to eat his ribbon.

Soon it was time for the big family dinner. Before eating, everyone in the Lewis family shared what each one loved most about family.

After dinner, Great Uncle Isaac began playing music and said, "Alright! It's time to celebrate!"

"Oh boy!" Andrew did a wiggle dance. "The moment I've been waiting for!"

The entire Lewis family participated as Andrew led the Electric Slide, his favorite line dance. Baby Aaron tried to dance, too, even though he couldn't walk yet.

It was another wonderful family reunion. Ana and Andrew couldn't wait to do it again next year. They looked forward to celebrating with their family for many years to come.